Dinosaur vs.

SANTA

BOB SHEA

Disney • Hyperion Books/New York

For information address Disney • Hyperion Books,
114 Fifth Avenue, New York, New York 10011-5690.

First Edition
10 9 8 7 6 5 4 3 2
H106-9333-5-13263
Printed in Malaysia

Reinforced binding

Library of Congress Cataloging-in-Publication Data
Shea, Bob.
Dinosaur vs. Santa / Bob Shea.—1st ed.
p. cm.
Summary: "Little Dinosaur gets ready for
Christmas"—Provided by publisher.
ISBN 978-1-4231-6806-5 (hardback)
[1. Christmas—Fiction. 2. Dinosaurs—Fiction.
3. Humorous stories.]
I. Title. II. Title: Dinosaur versus Santa.
PZ7.S53743DI 2012
[E]—dc23   2011051350

Visit www.disneyhyperionbooks.com

For Ryan

ROAR!

I'M A DINOSAUR!

roar!

roar! roar!

Dinosaur versus...

a letter to Santa!

DINOSAUR WINS!

SANtA
norTH pol e

roar!

roar!

roar!

Dinosaur versus…

decorating!

ROAR! ROAR! ROAR!

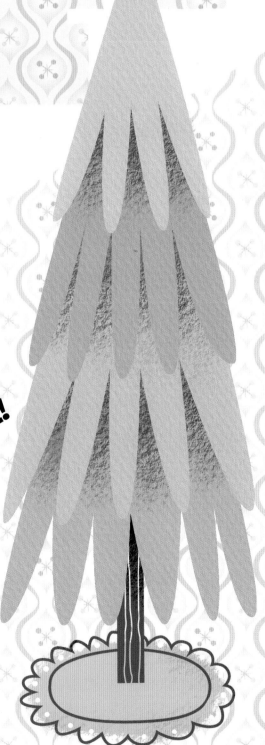

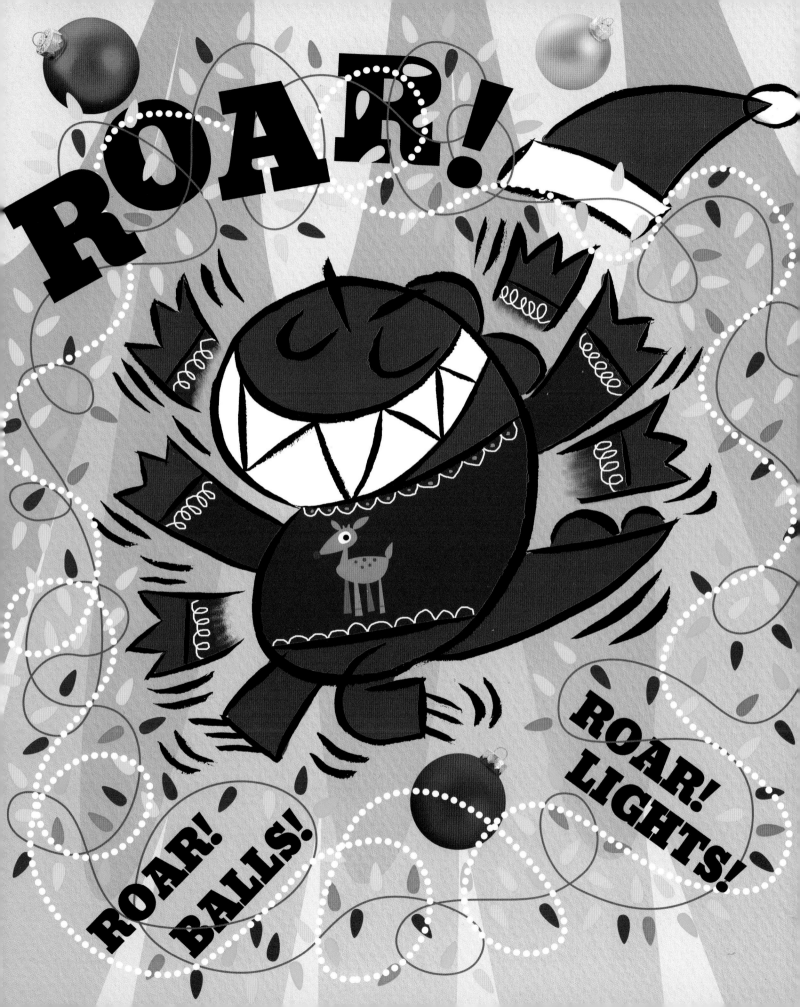

ROAR!

ROAR!

DINOSAUR WINS!

roar!

roar!

roar!

Dinosaur versus...

presents for Mom and Dad!

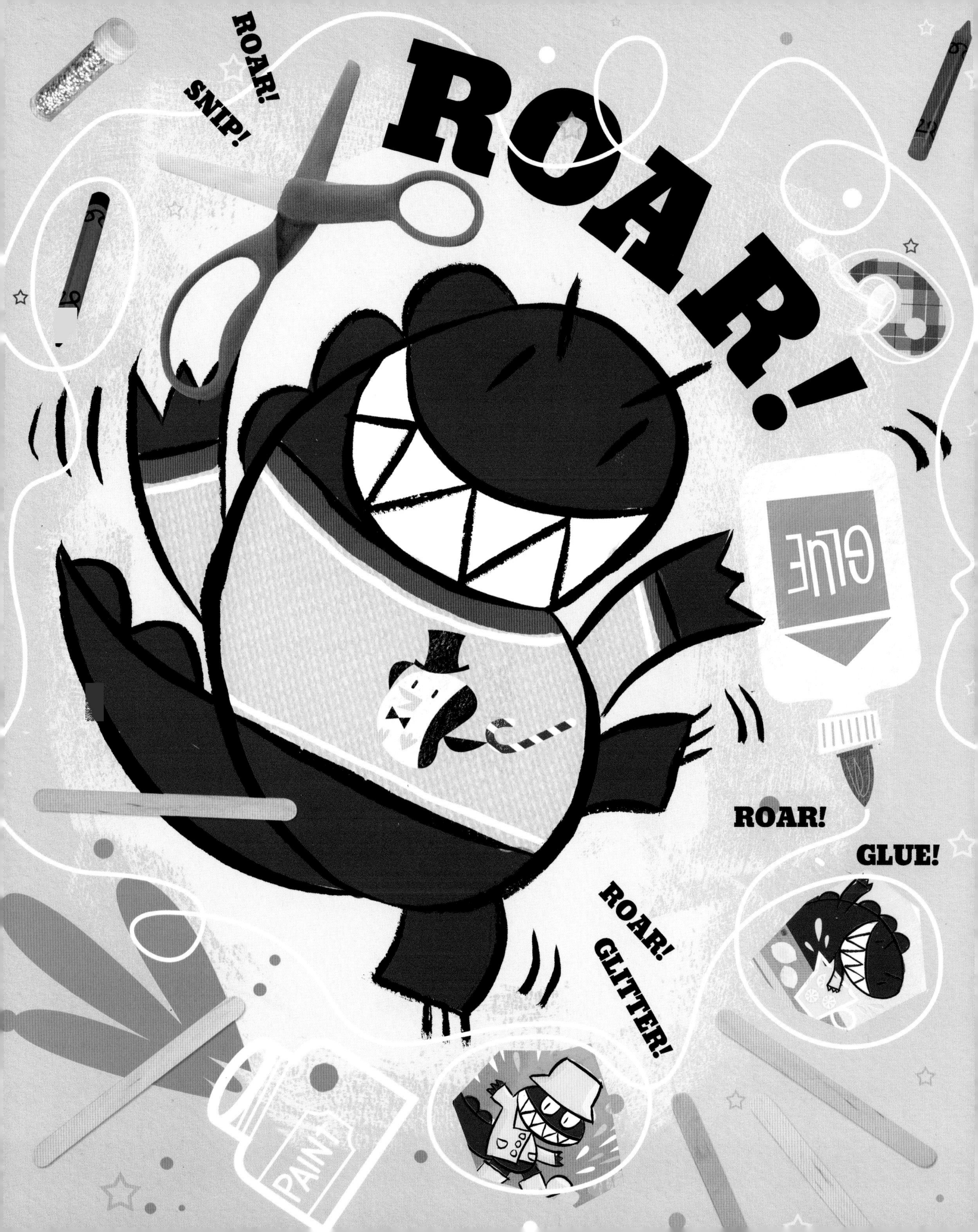
ROAR!
SNIP!
ROAR!
GLUE
ROAR!
GLUE!
ROAR!
GLITTER!
PAINT

roar!
roar!

Dinosaur versus...

being extra good!

ROAR!

ROAR!

roar?

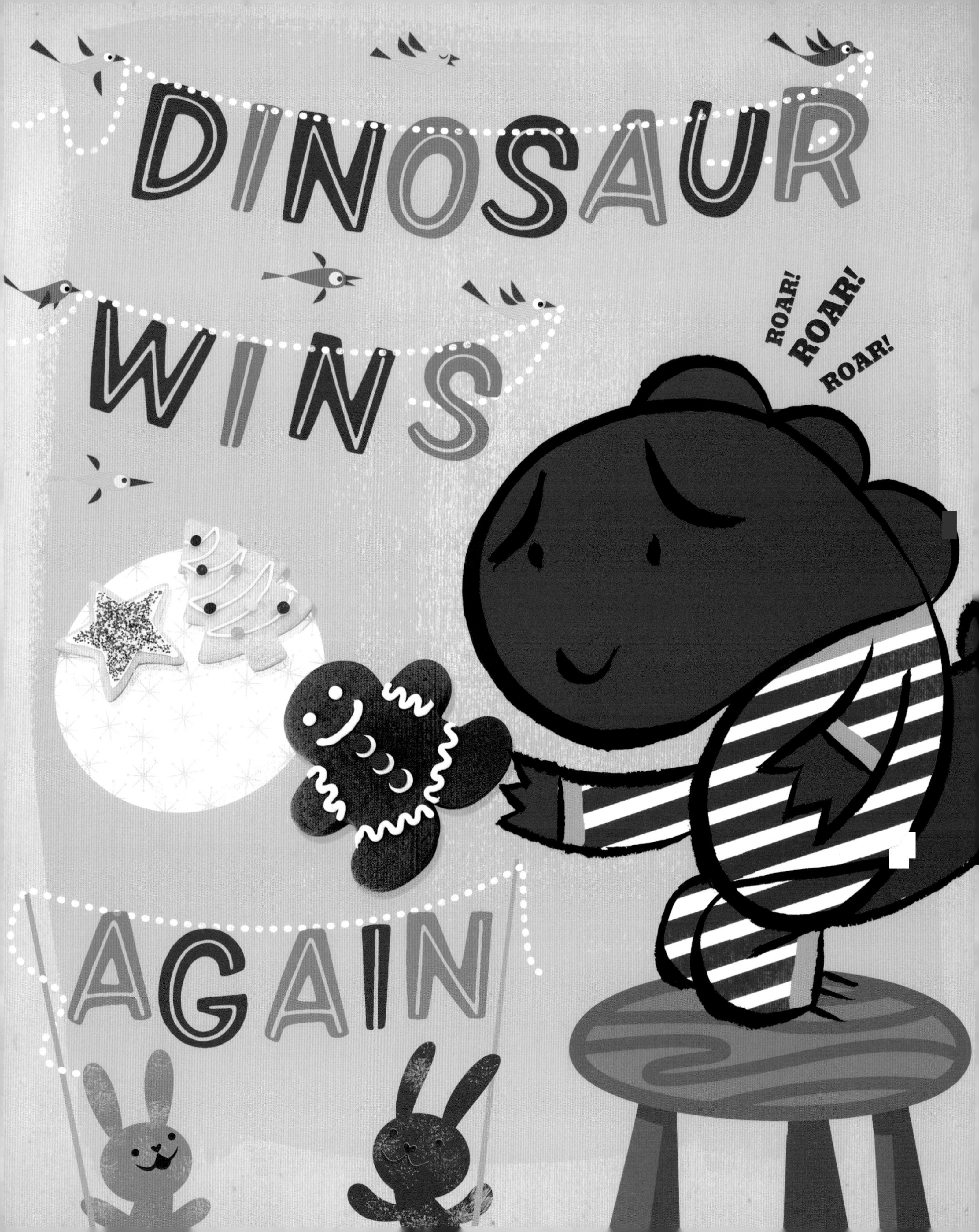
DINOSAUR WINS AGAIN
ROAR! ROAR! ROAR!

roar!

roar!

roar!

Dinosaur versus…

falling asleep on Christmas Eve!

roar! toss!

roar! turn!

drink! roar! stall!

roar! pee! potty! roar!

jingle

jingle   jingle

**Now Dinosaur will do something
no dinosaur should ever do . . .**

Oh no, Dinosaur!

Did Santa see you?   **Will he put you on the Naughty list?**

Will he take back all the presents?

ZZZZZZZZ

DINOSAUR WINS!

Merry Christmas, Dinosaur!